Written and Illustrated by
MARC BROWN

ARTHUR'S TEACHER MOVES IN

Based on a teleplay by Joe Fallon

Little, Brown and Company
Boston New York London

For my
third grade teacher, Miss Kingston –
little did I know my destiny while
sitting in row three

First Edition

Arthur® is a registered trademark of Marc Brown.

Library of Congress Cataloging-in-Publication Data

Brown, Marc Tolon.
    Arthur's teacher moves in / Marc Brown. — 1st ed.
      p.   cm. — (An Arthur adventure)
    "Adapted by Marc Brown from a teleplay by Joe Fallon."
    Summary: Arthur thinks that having his teacher stay at his house
will be a horrible experience.
    ISBN 0-316-11979-2 (hardcover)
    [1. Teachers — Fiction. 2. Schools — Fiction. 3. Aardvark —
Fiction. 4. Animals — Fiction.] I. Title
PZ7.B81618 Arqf 2000
[E] — dc21   99-043720

10 9 8 7 6 5 4 3 2 1

WOR

Printed in the United States of America

It was Friday afternoon, and Arthur was relaxing. "Whew . . . no Mr. Ratburn all weekend," Arthur said. "Arthur," said Mom, "I just heard some bad news. The snow collapsed Mr. Ratburn's roof, and he has nowhere to stay."

"Oh, too bad," Arthur said, his eyes glued to the TV.
"I knew you'd feel that way," his mother said. "So we invited him to stay here."
"Oh, okay," Arthur said, still watching TV.
"Stay HERE???" Arthur ran after Mom.

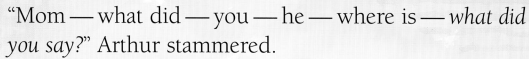

"Mom — what did — you — he — where is — *what did you say?*" Arthur stammered.

"Arthur's teacher is going to stay here!" sang D.W.

"Just until his roof is fixed," said Mom.

Arthur couldn't believe it.

Later that day, Arthur told Buster the news.
"It's too weird," Arthur said. "My teacher in my house, walking on my carpet, eating from my spoons, and touching my stuff!"
Buster agreed. "School is at school and home is at home because that's the way it's supposed to be."
"Exactly!" Arthur nodded.

But his parents didn't understand.

"It's just plain wrong," Arthur tried to explain. "It goes against nature!"

"The poor man has nowhere else to go," said Dad.

"He's going to stay here," said Mom, "and we're *all* going to make him feel welcome."

Arthur tried to imagine Mr. Ratburn staying at his house, but the picture in his head was too horrible.

The next day, Arthur borrowed books from the Brain and rushed home to put up new posters.
"What are you doing?" asked D.W.
"You wouldn't understand," Arthur answered.
"Are you trying to make Mr. Ragworm think you're smarter than you really are?"
"Go away," Arthur said.
Then the doorbell rang.

"Arthur! D.W.!" called Mom. "Come say hello!"
"Hi, Mr. Ratbite," said D.W. "Is it true you torture kids?"
"Here I am!" Arthur cried. "Welcome! Hello! Come in!"
"Please take these up to your room, Arthur," said Dad.
"He's staying in Arthur's room!" sang D.W.
"I put your sleeping bag in D.W.'s room," said Mom.
"Hey, no fair!" said D.W.

Mr. Ratburn saw the books on Arthur's table.
"Those are my favorite books in the whole world,"
Arthur said.
"Hmmm," Mr. Ratburn said. "*Trigonometry for Fun . . .
The Double Helix and You . . .*"
"Didn't you just borrow those from the Brain?" said
D.W.
"I use my *brain* a lot," Arthur said quickly.

"Mr. Ropeburns," said D.W., "look what's under
here. . . ."
Arthur quickly leaned against the poster. "I think
I smell Dad making a cake," he said.
"Cake!" said D.W. She ran out the door.
"Cake?" said Mr. Ratburn. He ran out, too.
Arthur sank onto his bed, relieved.

Later, Arthur was watching *The Bionic Bunny Show*. But when Mr. Ratburn came into the room, Arthur quickly changed the channel.

"You look . . . different," Arthur said.

"I don't always dress for school," said Mr. Ratburn.

"Mr. Rathead," said D.W., "you were lucky you weren't in school when the roof fell in."

"It was the roof to my home," said Mr. Ratburn.

D.W. looked confused.

"Teachers don't live at school," Mr. Ratburn explained. "We have houses just like you do."

"Oh," said D.W. "The world was so simple until now."

"Would you like to watch one of my videos?"
Mr. Ratburn asked Arthur.
"Of course," said Arthur. "I *love* educational videos."
A cartoon kangaroo appeared on the screen.
"*Spooky Poo*?" Arthur said.
"One of my favorites!" said Mr. Ratburn.

After *Spooky Poo,* Mr. Ratburn covered Arthur's history
book with a handkerchief and waved his hand over it.
When he pulled the handkerchief away, the book was
gone!
"Shazam! No homework tonight!"
"Wow!" said Arthur. "Can you teach me that?"
"Sure," Mr. Ratburn said.

For dessert, Dad brought out a huge cake.
"I like it when Mr. Ragburp stays with us," said D.W.

On Monday morning, Arthur's friends all shook their
heads.
"Can you imagine Ratburn living with you?" said Buster.
"I bet Arthur's ready to run away," said Francine.
"Hey, Arthur," said Buster, "you can stay at my house
until Ratburn goes home."
"It's not so bad," said Arthur. "He taught me a magic
trick. We had fun."
Mr. Ratburn waved at Arthur. Arthur waved back.

At lunch, everyone was talking about the math test.
"I got a C minus," Buster said.
"You beat me," Muffy said.
"Arthur got an A," said Francine. "It's not fair!"
"Yeah, *we* could all get A's if Mr. Ratburn lived with *us* and *our* fathers made cakes for him," said Muffy.
"But I studied hard for that test!" Arthur protested.
"Sure you did," everyone said.

After school, all of Arthur's friends were busy.
"Want to watch some *Spooky Poo*?" Arthur asked.
"I don't think so," said Buster. "I don't want to get
between you and your new *friend*."

"Want to go to the Sugar Bowl for some hot cocoa?"
Arthur asked Francine and Muffy.
Francine shook her head. "Sorry. We're already going to
the Sugar Bowl for some hot cocoa."

Then the Brain asked for his books back.
"Sure," said Arthur. "I'll bring them to your house."
"No thanks. Please bring them to school," said the Brain.

"Teacher's pet, teacher's pet," sang Binky. "That means you, Arthur!" Then he handed Arthur a note from Fern. Arthur walked home alone.

Pal was at the door to greet him.
"It's great to get home," said Arthur, "and forget all about school."

Mr. Ratburn was at the kitchen table, eating cake.
"Oh," said Arthur. "Hi." He quickly left the room.

Later, Arthur showed Fern's drawing to his parents and Mr. Ratburn.

"And Binky called me a teacher's pet," Arthur said.

"Maybe I should talk to everyone," said Mr. Ratburn.

"No!" Arthur said. "That will make it worse!"

"You know I wouldn't give you special treatment," Mr. Ratburn said. "And you *have* studied hard lately."

"If you give me an F," said Arthur, "that'll prove I'm not a teacher's pet."

"Soon they'll realize that they're wrong," said Mom.

"Not as soon as if he gave me an F," said Arthur.

Tuesday at lunch, everyone made fun of Arthur.
"Teacher's pet, teacher's pet," sang Binky.
"If cake gets you one A, will apple pie get you two A's?"
said Francine.
"Maybe with some vanilla ice cream on top," said Muffy.
Arthur tried to laugh.

Mr. Ratburn walked over.

"Arthur, I won't be staying at your house anymore."

"Really?" said Arthur.

Mr. Ratburn nodded. "I need to be closer to my house to supervise the work on my roof, so . . .

"Francine's parents have invited me to stay with them. After that, I'll be staying at Binky's house. Who knows?" said Mr. Ratburn as he walked away. "I may also stay at Muffy's, Buster's, Fern's . . ."

FIC $15.95
BRO   Brown, Marc
        Arthur's Teacher Moves In